Pet
Parade

A POLK STREET SPECIAL

Pet
Parade

. . . .

Patricia Reilly Giff
Illustrated by Blanche Sims

A Yearling Book

Published by
Bantam Doubleday Dell Books for Young Readers
a division of
Bantam Doubleday Dell Publishing Group, Inc.
1540 Broadway
New York, New York 10036

ISBN: 0-440-41232-3
Printed in the United States of America
September 1996
10 9 8 7 6 5 4 3 2 1
CWO

To J. R. Fiddle,
elegant gentleman,
spectacular cat

Chapter 1

Outside, it was pouring.

Inside, Ms. Rooney had turned on the lights.

Beast took a deep breath.

Everything smelled like wet boots and socks.

He loved that smell.

He loved a rainy-day classroom.

He wiggled his bare toes.

His socks were hanging on the window-sill.

That was the best part of all.

He could get out of his seat a thousand times to see if they were dry.

They never were.

He had stamped in a puddle as big as a whale.

Ms. Rooney's class was studying whales right now.

And other sea creatures.

They were studying land creatures too.

"What do you think, Richard?" Ms. Rooney asked.

"Whales are good," Beast said.

Everyone laughed.

"Not whales," said Ms. Rooney. "Hermit crabs."

Too bad he hadn't heard one word Ms. Rooney was saying.

He had never heard of hermit crabs in his whole life.

Timothy Barbiero knew all about them, though.

He was talking a hundred miles a minute, about their eight skinny little legs . . . and how they move to bigger shells as they grow.

Beast wished he were as smart as Timothy.

Half as smart.

Even a smidge as smart.

He listened to the class talking about creatures for a while. Sherri Dent was talking about ladybugs, and Derrick Grace was talking about mice.

Then Beast went over to the radiator to check his socks.

Ms. Rooney was talking about someone named Mr. Schaeffer.

"He's the best cat I ever had," she said. "Someday you'll have to meet him."

Beast stared out the window. It looked as if raindrops were bombing the puddles in the schoolyard.

"Pshuum-baaaah!" he said under his breath.

Something was going on behind him.

Everyone was clapping.

Beast went back to his seat. He began to draw a picture of a cat named Mr. Schaeffer.

Up in front, Ms. Rooney was smiling. "Noah Greene," she said, "that's the best idea you ever had."

Noah was smart too, Beast thought. Much smarter than he was.

Beast began to draw a picture of Noah.

He was sick of Noah with his great ideas all the time.

Too bad he didn't know what Noah's idea was.

Any minute Ms. Rooney might ask him something about it.

Ms. Rooney was talking about dogs now.

Beast drew a picture of his dog, Kissie Poo.

Kissie Poo was taking a little bite out of Noah's leg.

Beast would draw Timothy next.

Let Kissie Poo give him a nip too.

Beast started to laugh.

Kissie Poo had about three teeth.

Everyone was clapping now.

Everyone but Jill Simon.

She looked as if she were going to cry.

"Yes," said Ms. Rooney. "We'll all bring our pets. It will be Pet Week in Room 113."

Jill really was crying now. "All I have is

a teeny little goldfish." She sniffed. "And he really isn't very gold."

But Timothy was smiling. "Wait till you see what I've got."

"Me too," said Noah.

Beast thought about bringing Kissie Poo to school.

Kissie Poo was the boringest dog in the world. All she did was eat and sleep . . . eat and sleep.

He picked up his pencil again.

He drew an X over Timothy and Noah.

He drew one over Kissie Poo too.

Chapter 2

It had stopped raining by the time Beast got home.

His socks were still wet, though.

They made his toes stick together.

His mother was in the kitchen cooking a mess of green stuff.

Green stuff he hated.

It was her day off.

She smiled at him. "Homework first," she said.

He didn't have time for homework.

He had had a great idea on the way home. Just as good as any of Noah's.

"Before I even change my socks?" he asked. "They're sopping wet."

His mother sighed. "Yes. Change your socks."

He thought about his idea again.

Suppose he could teach Kissie Poo a bunch of tricks for Pet Week?

Beast went up to his bedroom. He dragged his knapsack behind him.

Kissie Poo was snoring under the bed.

Beast felt the tops of his socks.

Not so wet.

It would be the worst nuisance to change them.

His sneaker laces were all knotted.

He sat down on the floor.

Tricks.

Yes.

Timothy and Noah would be asking him how he had done it.

Maybe he'd show them.

Maybe not.

But what tricks?

Rolling over?

Not so hot.

Kissie Poo had no hair on her stomach. She was all fat and pink.

Gross.

How would it be if she carried his backpack into the classroom instead?

He'd snap his fingers. She'd drop the backpack in front of his desk.

Maybe he could teach her to open it.

She could take out his books, his pencils, his lunch.

He looped his bedspread up over the bed and peered underneath.

Kissie Poo was curled up in back with a pile of junk . . . Beast's old army men and the dustballs.

Beast clicked his tongue. "Here, girl."

She thumped her tail once to say hello.

Beast reached under the bed as far as he could. Kissie Poo gave a warning growl.

Sometimes Kissie Poo was a little testy.

"Stop that," Beast said in a loud voice.

"Mother!" his sister, Holly, yelled from her bedroom. "Beast is torturing Kissie Poo."

"I am not!" he shouted at the top of his lungs.

"We picked that poor dog out to give her a good life, you know!" Holly screeched.

Beast thought back to the day they had gotten her.

He had seen a huge German shepherd. He had seen a tough-looking spotted dog.

Perfect.

Then his mother had seen Kissie Poo.

"No one will take this one," she had said.

"You're right," Beast had told her.

Kissie Poo was fat with bulging eyes. Her tongue stuck out over her three teeth.

She was the saddest-looking dog Beast had ever seen.

"Poor dog," Holly had said.

The man had opened the cage. "Her name is Kissie Poo," he said. "She's not happy. She never even sleeps."

Before Beast could say a word, Kissie Poo was his. She had sat in his lap all the way home, sound asleep.

"She's happy now," his mother said.

Right now, Kissie Poo opened one bulging eye.

"Come on out here," Beast whispered. "I'm going to teach you a great trick."

He was still reaching.

He could feel the end of her tail.

Still too far to grab.

Now Holly was at his bedroom door. "You can be arrested for being mean to animals," she said. "I saw that on TV."

Beast lunged for Kissie Poo.

She snapped her three teeth.

"Yeow!" Beast yelled.

"Serves you right," Holly said.

Beast narrowed his eyes. "I think you forgot something."

"I didn't forget anything." Holly started back down the hall.

"You forgot it's your birthday in a couple of days," he said.

If Holly thought he was going to get her a birthday present . . .

Holly didn't answer.

Beast took another look at Kissie Poo.

He sighed.

She was sound asleep again.

He'd never be able to teach her tricks.

Never.

Chapter 3

It was the next day after school.

Beast was lying on the kitchen floor. He had to write a story about pets.

He looked up. Holly was sitting at the table.

She was looking through a fat book . . . a dictionary. "Listen to this," she said. "*Em-por-i-um*. It means a store."

She smiled. "I just love big words."

Beast wasn't smiling.

He hated to write.

"How do you spell *rattlesnake*?" he asked.

"That's so easy," she said. "Besides, if you just looked it up in the dictionary . . ."

He didn't bother with the dictionary.

He wrote *ratel sneak.*

Holly was looking over his shoulder. "Wrong," she said. "Wrong as usual."

Behind them was a noise.

Pa-boom!

"Good grief," Holly said. "Someone's trying to break the door down."

"It's Matthew." Beast threw his pet story into his backpack. It was good enough.

All about a kid who had a pet rattler.

He reached for the doorknob and opened the door for Matthew Jackson. "Come on in," he said. "I'll get rid of Olly-Hay."

"Ood-Gay," Matthew said.

It was their new secret language. It was the easiest thing in the world.

All you had to do was . . .

"I know what you're saying, Ichard-Ray," Holly said. "You think I was born two minutes ago?"

Maybe the new language was too easy, he thought.

They'd have to find a way to make it harder.

He took Matthew upstairs to his room.

Kissie Poo was snoring under the bed.

That reminded Beast.

"Are you going to bring Barney?" he asked.

Matthew frowned.

"For Pet Week," Beast said.

"I know what you mean." Matthew looked out the window. "Barney's a great cat," he said, "but she doesn't do much."

Beast nodded.

Kissie Poo's tail was hanging out from under the bedspread.

There were about four hairs on her tail.

Beast's father had said that she might have been in a fight.

Maybe a cat had chewed up her tail.

Matthew lay on the floor. "I heard Noah is bringing a ferret."

A ferret. Wouldn't you know, Beast thought.

He pushed Kissie Poo's tail under the spread. He could hear her snarl a little.

Sometimes she was just like Holly.

Beast thought about Timothy.

Timothy was probably going to bring something great.

Beast pictured him walking into Room 113 with a lion on a leash, or maybe a . . .

Matthew was frowning again. "Timothy will probably bring a—"

"Bengal tiger," Beast said.

"Iger-Tay." Matthew started to laugh. Then he stopped. "I'm not bringing Barney." He shook his head. "Definitely not."

Beast tried to think of how to say it in their new language. "Efinitely-Day ot-nay," he said.

Everyone would be laughing if he brought Kissie Poo. He could see her snarling with her three teeth. He could see her tail without hair.

And what about that ridiculous name?

He'd have to change it.

"Here, Rattlesnake," he said. "Here . . ."

He could hear Holly rooting around in her bedroom.

She was moving furniture.

Screech went the bed as she shoved it across the floor.

Clunk went her dresser.

Matthew looked up. "What's that kid doing, anyway?"

"She wants her room to look just right for her new fish tank."

"What fish tank?" Matthew asked.

Beast raised one shoulder in the air.

"Her birthday's tomorrow," he said. "She asked my mother and father for a fish tank. She wants me to buy the fish."

That Holly. She had bottles of water all over her room. She was saving them for the tank.

"You have to have old water," she had told him. "I read it in a fish book."

Matthew leaned over. "What's that sticking out . . . ?"

It was Kissie Poo's tail.

Beast shoved it under the bed again.

"Come on," he told Matthew. "Let's go get Holly a fish."

He slapped his pocket for money. Not one cent.

He reached under his bed.

He could hear Kissie Poo growling as he pulled out a couple of quarters.

"Too bad I don't have enough money for a man-eating octopus," he said.

Chapter 4

It was the next afternoon.
Beast closed his closet door all the way.
He threw a pile of socks and underwear in front.

Holly wouldn't move all that junk to search in his closet.

Not in a million years.

He stood there thinking.

Inside the closet were two little bags filled with water.

One bag had a brown-tailed pencilfish.

The other had a rummy-nose.

They were the greatest fish in the world. Even Timothy and Noah couldn't have picked better.

Beast could hear Matthew. "East-Bay!" he screeched at the top of his lungs.

They were going to the park.

Beast took a step toward the hall.

The fish probably hated it in the closet. They probably hated the dark.

Maybe he could leave the closet door open a speck.

"I'm going!" Matthew yelled. "I'm going right this minute."

Beast yanked open his closet door. He grabbed up the two bags of fish. "Don't worry," he said. "You're coming with me."

He slid down the hall on tiptoe.

Holly was moving furniture again. She must think she was getting a fish tank the size of an elephant.

Beast had seen the tank in his mother's closet. It was the size of a pea.

Just big enough for a pencilfish and a rummy-nose.

"Is that you, Beast?" Holly yelled.

"No!" he yelled. He dived down the stairs.

"Very funny," she called after him.

He raced out the door with a fish bag in each hand.

Matthew was sitting on the curb. "I've only been waiting about an hour," he said.

He looked up at Beast. "How do you think we're going to be able to hunt if we're carrying those fish all over?"

Beast handed him one of the bags.

"We'll think of something," he said. "Let's just get out of here before Osy-Nay Olly-Hay looks out the window."

They rushed down the street.

"I left the stuff we need there already. On a bench," Matthew said. "A pail. A tea-spoon. I couldn't find a shovel."

Beast didn't bother to answer. He was out of breath. Besides, he wanted to keep the water in the bags straight.

He didn't want Leady or Rummy to get dizzy from being jostled around.

Leady. A great name for a pencilfish. And Rummy wasn't bad for a rummy-nose.

He was going to tell Holly. If she was smart, she'd keep those names.

The park was cool, shady. A million red leaves were drifting off the trees.

He and Matthew headed for the back.

They looked around for a good place to leave the fish.

"Here," he told Matthew. "Under this tree. Much better than a dark closet."

They set the fish down carefully and watched them for a minute.

"All right," Beast said. "Let's get started."

He reached for the pail. "We'll take a little walk. In no time—"

Just then Dawn Bosco and Jill ran past.

They didn't even stop to say hello.

Beast and Matthew looked after them.

"Why is Jill wearing that net thing over her head?" Beast asked.

"We've got to get lots of dirt," Matthew was saying. "Make them feel at home."

"Soil . . . ," said Beast. "That's what the TV program said last night."

Matthew leaned in close to Beast.

"I think you've saved our lives with this idea," he said. "No one will ever think of bringing ants for Pet Week."

"An ant farm." Beast had heard those words on television last night too. That's where he'd gotten the idea.

A nature program had been on. It had shown a man who had an ant farm in his house.

Skillions of ants. All of them rushing around in tunnels in a glass fish tank.

"There." Beast pointed to an anthill.

He felt good. Great.

Too bad about Noah and Timothy.

He'd learned a pack of other stuff last night too.

All about how hard ants work. All about how they take care of the queen and the baby ants.

They knelt down to watch.

"See," Beast said, "they're made of three lumps. The head, and two other parts. I forget what they're called. They have six legs, anyway."

"Out of my way!" someone yelled.

Beast looked up.

Wayne O'Brien was hopping over their pail.

Wayne kept going. "I'm getting myself an ant farm," he called back. "Best pets in the world."

He disappeared behind a tree.

Beast sat back. "I guess Wayne watched the same television program."

Matthew nodded. "I bet Dawn and Jill did too."

Beast sighed. "That's why Jill was wearing a net. She's probably afraid of ants."

He watched the anthill. Ants were carrying tiny crumbs into their den.

"Everyone in the class is going to have an ant farm," Matthew said.

Beast shook his head. "Not us." And probably not Timothy and Noah, he thought.

"Efinitely-Day ot-nay," said Matthew.

Chapter 5

Someone was singing.

Beast could hear it even though he was sure he was still asleep.

Kissie Poo could hear it too.

She growled in her sleep and curled up closer to Beast.

One thing about Kissie Poo.

She always slept in Beast's bed, never in Holly's.

Another thing, Beast thought, still half asleep.

Kissie Poo had great ears.

They were soft and silky.

Beast liked to run his fingers over them.

The singing began again.

It was Holly.

Why was she up so early?

Beast could hear her moving around.

He sat up and listened.

"Happy Birthday."

She was singing "Happy Birthday" to herself.

That Holly was razy-cay.

He tugged Kissie Poo's ears and waited while she licked his hand with her fat tongue.

Suddenly he thought of something.

The most wonderful idea.

He jumped out of bed.

He dashed down to Holly's room. "Happy Birthday," he said.

Holly smiled and said, "How about my presents?"

"That's what I want to ask you," he said. "Could I borrow—"

Already Holly was shaking her head.

Beast rushed on. "—borrow your birthday fish for Pet Week?"

"Absolutely not—" she began, and saw his face.

"Then I won't give—" he said.

"All right," she said. "Make sure you don't lose them."

"I never lose anything," he said.

He went back down the hall.

He was bringing the two greatest fish in the world for Pet Week.

He'd share with Matthew, of course.

One each.

Holly was pounding down the stairs.

"Present time!" she was yelling.

Beast threw on his clothes. He went into the kitchen.

Everyone was at the table already.

Holly held her hand out. "Hand them over," she said.

"That's not so nice," her father said.

"Please," Holly said.

"Open the big one first," said their mother. "The one from us."

Holly ripped open the red-and-white-striped package on the table.

"A fish tank," she said. "It's the best surprise I ever had."

She kissed her mother and father.

"It may be a little small," she said. "Just a tiny bit . . ."

"There's more," said her mother.

Holly opened two other boxes.

One had a dictionary. It was even fatter than her old one.

"I'm in love with dictionaries," she told them.

Yucks, thought Beast.

The other had pink underwear with dots.

Double yucks.

"Excellent." Holly looked at Beast. "Your turn."

Beast looked back at her. "My turn?"

And then he remembered.

Triple yucks.

The fish.

He hadn't brought them home. They'd been out in the park all night.

He'd have to get himself right over there before school this morning.

He wouldn't even have time for breakfast.

"Richard?" Holly was asking.

He shook his head. "I'm giving them to you tonight."

He shoved a piece of English muffin in his mouth, swallowed a half glass of juice, and was out the door.

"Richard," his mother called. "Don't forget . . ."

He didn't stop.

He went to the park as fast as he could.

He wondered how long fish could go without food.

At least they had plenty of water, he thought, trying to cheer himself up. They could drink as much as they wanted.

No one was in the park.

Beast stopped to take a breath.

He had a stitch in his side from running.

He walked a little more slowly, trying to remember. They had put the fish under a tree.

But which one?

He wandered around the park for a long time.

The fish weren't anywhere.

He looked up.

It was really quiet. No one was walking toward school.

Good grief, he said to himself, and started to run.

It wasn't until he reached Room 113 that he remembered.

He had left his books at home. And his homework too.

But worse yet, his lunch.

Chapter 6

Everyone was in the classroom ahead of him.

Beast went toward his seat. He thought about the poor fish.

Maybe someone had stepped on them.

Maybe leaves had fallen and covered them overnight.

Maybe he'd never know what had happened to them.

And what could he tell Holly?

He tripped over someone's feet.

"Watch where you're going," Dawn said in a fresh voice.

He took a breath. He wanted to say "Keep your feet under your seat."

He was too worried about the fish to bother.

He looked down at Dawn's desk.

She was writing a story.

He could see the words:

THE LUCKIEST DAY OF MY LIFE

Dawn slammed her hand over it. "Private," she said.

Up in front Linda Lorca was yelling: "Anyone need a pet for Pet Week? I have caterpillars for sale. Two for ten cents. Cages a nickel."

"They must be some cages," Dawn said.

Linda didn't answer. She just sniffed. She began again. "Pets for sale . . ."

Too bad Holly wasn't crazy about cater-pillars, Beast thought.

He looked around. He didn't see Mat-thew.

He needed Matthew to save his life.

Maybe he was in the coat closet.

Beast rushed to the closet doors.

Matthew was swinging on a shelf.

"My fish." Beast could hardly get the words out. "Did you see . . ."

Matthew's mouth opened in a wide O. "We forgot all about them. Left the poor guys out in the cold . . ."

"Is everybody ready?" Ms. Rooney was calling. "It's time for lunch money, and I have a surprise."

Matthew took a flying leap out of the closet.

"Wait," Beast said. "The other thing I wanted to ask. Do you have a lot of lunch?"

Matthew didn't say anything.

"Extra lunch?" Beast said. "Maybe we could share."

Matthew's mouth opened wide again. "I forgot my lunch. It was peanut butter and onions."

"Yuck," said Beast. "Matthew, how could you . . ." He looked up.

Ms. Rooney was frowning. "I'm waiting patiently."

Beast knew she wasn't going to be patient much longer.

He started for his seat.

He could see Jill Simon crying at her desk.

"No lunch money?" he asked.

She shook her head. "Dawn isn't going to be an ant farmer with me anymore. She has two other pets."

Jill cried harder. "I can't even touch those ants."

Ms. Rooney was still frowning. She waited for Beast to slide into his seat.

"Here's the news," Ms. Rooney said. "Mr. Mancina is excited about Pet Week. He's going to give us a Cavia."

She wrote it on the board.

Then she smiled. "He's giving a prize to the one who figures out what that is."

Beast looked around.

Timothy, or Noah. Of course.

They didn't raise their hands. No one did.

"Keep thinking," Ms. Rooney said. "Now, hot-lunch money."

Half the class raced up to her desk.

Beast tapped Matthew on the back. "Do you have any money?"

Matthew shook his head. "Sorry," he said.

Beast tried to think whether he could go a whole day without eating.

He had never done that in his life.

"Chocolate milk, plain milk, dessert," Ms. Rooney was calling.

Beast leaned over. "Hey, Emily. How about lending me a dime?"

Emily Arrow shook her head. "Sorry, I don't have any."

"Home-lunch people, names on the blackboard," said Ms. Rooney.

Beast watched Matthew get up.

"You're going home?" Beast asked.

Lucky Matthew.

Beast's mother had gone to work.

So had his father.

Matthew wrote his name in large letters. MATTHEW J. JACKSON.

Then he slid back into his seat again. "I'm not going home," he whispered to Beast. "But I'm not going to sit in the cafeteria and watch the whole world eat."

Beast stood up. He wrote his name under Matthew's.

He wasn't going to watch the whole world eat either.

Chapter 7

It was strange to be out at lunchtime, Beast thought.

Matthew must have thought so too. "What are we going to do?" he asked.

Beast felt the key that was looped on a string around his neck.

"We could go to my house," he said.

He knew it was a mistake the moment he said it.

His mother would have a fit if she found out that he hadn't waited for Holly.

He and Matthew walked toward his house.

Matthew didn't think it was a mistake.

He slapped Beast on the back. "Terrific idea. What do you have to eat?"

Beast thought about it. "Peanut butter, I guess. Jelly. Maybe some bologna."

"Onions?" Matthew asked.

"Yes." Beast walked slowly around the back.

He put his key in the lock and went into the kitchen.

"Cool," Matthew said. "We should do this every day."

Not so cool, Beast thought.

"Will your mother mind?" Matthew asked.

"Of course not," Beast said.

Just then the phone rang. Once, twice.

Beast pulled out the jar of peanut butter.

The phone was ringing in his ear. He made believe he wasn't paying attention.

He went to the refrigerator for the bologna.

"Aren't you going to answer that?" Matthew asked.

Beast shook his head. "It's probably just some pest."

He could feel his heart pounding.

Maybe his mother had found out he was home.

Maybe she was calling to say he was in big trouble.

He heard a sound at the kitchen door and jumped.

Kissie Poo was standing there.

She was hungry.

Kissie Poo was always hungry.

"Kissie Poo's getting fat," Matthew said.

"You're right," Beast said.

Kissie Poo wagged her tail at Beast.

She was dying for a piece of bologna.

"Maybe you shouldn't give her anything," Matthew said. "Maybe she'll get too fat."

Beast swallowed.

Kissie Poo loved bologna.

She was looking up at him with her bulging brown eyes.

She couldn't believe he wasn't going to give her any.

Beast shook his head at her. "No good," he said.

The phone stopped ringing at last.

It's just a pest, he told himself. Don't worry.

He watched Matthew make a fat sand-

wich. Peanut butter, a slice of bologna, and half an onion.

"What are you going to have?" Matthew asked.

Beast thought about the phone. He wouldn't be able to eat anything.

Maybe he'd never eat again.

"I'm not so hungry," he told Matthew.

Matthew took a huge bite of sandwich. "Then let's go back," he said. "We can play Keep-away in the schoolyard."

Beast nodded. He let Matthew go out the door first.

He made believe he didn't hear Kissie Poo crying.

He started to run.

He could hear the phone begin to ring again.

Chapter 8

Everyone was standing at the science table.

Alex Walker had brought in his hamster
and her five little babies.

They were curled up in their cage on a
pile of cedar chips.

"My mother says we can give the babies
away when they grow up," Alex said.

"How do they get along with dogs?" Beast asked.

Alex shook his head. "Not so good, I think. But you can keep them in their cage."

Beast went back to his seat, thinking about it.

He was beginning to be hungry again.

He fished around in his desk and found an old Life Saver.

It tasted great, even though the paper was stuck to it.

Dawn was at her seat too. He could see her working on her story: MY LUCKIEST DAY.

She was doing the illustrations now.

A couple of skinny fish in a tank.

She was putting in lots of long, skinny green leaves too.

He leaned over. "Not bad," he said.

She looked up. "Thanks."

He watched her putting waves on the top of the tank.

"What do you think?" she asked.

"Nice," he said.

Not nice. She had just ruined the whole thing.

Alex was telling the rest of the class about the hamsters.

"They love apples and lettuce," he was saying.

Beast didn't care about lettuce, but his mouth watered when he thought about apples . . . apple pie, candy apples . . .

He fished in his desk again. No Life Savers were left.

He thought about Kissie Poo. The poor dog must be wondering why he hadn't fed her.

Dawn had picked up an orange crayon. She outlined LUCKIEST.

She drew a star over DAY.

She wrote TETRA on the bottom.

Beast leaned over. "What does your luckiest day have to do with fish?"

At that moment the bell rang. It was time for gym.

Dawn was out of her seat and first in line in two seconds.

Alex was still talking. "You have to watch out for hamsters," he said. "If you leave the cage door open, they'll escape."

Beast waited for Matthew before he started for the line. They liked to be last.

Something was bothering Beast.

He thought about it all the way to the gym.

Something more than being in trouble over lunch.

Something even worse than losing the fish.

What was it?

Something Alex had said had reminded him. It was something about keeping the hamster cage door closed.

He stopped.

Matthew bumped into him.

He had just thought of it. And it *was* worse than anything else.

Had he closed his back door after lunch?

He couldn't remember.

Suppose Kissie Poo had gotten out?

Suppose she was wandering around in the street?

Lost.

Run over.

The class marched into the gym.

It took forever to race up and down the gym.

And forever for the afternoon to be over.

If only he hadn't forgotten his lunch. If only—

"Pay attention, Richard," Ms. Rooney said.

That was the whole trouble, he thought.

He didn't pay attention to anything.

That's why the fish were gone, and Kissie Poo. And that's why he was going to be in trouble for going home for lunch.

He packed his books while Ms. Rooney gave out homework sheets. He was the first one out the door when the bell rang . . . even ahead of Dawn.

He was glad to see Holly waiting on the school steps. "We have to find Kissie Poo," he said.

Holly didn't bother to ask him a million questions.

"Let's go," she said.

They started to run.

Chapter 9

Kissie Poo was sitting on the back steps. She thumped her tail when she saw them.

Beast swallowed. "Good dog," he said.

He leaned over to pet her ears. He didn't want Holly to see he was going to cry.

"You don't need the key," Beast told her. "The door is open."

Holly put her hands on her hips. "I can

guess that. I wasn't born two minutes ago."

She shoved open the door.

Beast waited for Kissie Poo to walk inside.

Then he went in too. He headed straight for the refrigerator.

"Here comes bologna," he told the dog. "As much as you want."

Holly was talking the whole time. "You'd better tell me what's going on," she was saying. "The door was open. The poor dog was outside. And you've got tears all over the place . . ."

"I do not . . . ," he began, and stopped.

He told her the whole thing. The fish. His lunch. Matthew.

"You'd better take some of that bologna for yourself," she said. "Before you starve to death."

She said it nicely, though.

It made Beast want to cry again.

"I'm going to start over," he said. "I'm going to pay attention to everything."

Holly frowned. "I wonder what I'm going to do with an empty fish tank and all that water?" she was saying.

"I'm going to do my pet story over," he said. "I'm even going to look up *rattlesnake*."

"You can use my dictionary," she said. "Try not to lose it."

Holly wasn't bad sometimes, he thought. Not bad at all.

He sat down at the table.

He ate some of Kissie Poo's leftover bologna.

Then he pulled out his pet story.

It was a mess.

Never mind.

He was going to do the whole thing over anyway.

He opened Holly's dictionary.

It took a long time to find the *R*s.

Luckily there was a picture of a rattle-snake.

Underneath was a picture of a fish.

It looked like a rummy-nose.

He couldn't believe it. "Rummy-nose tetra," it said.

He had seen that other word somewhere. *Tetra.*

He sat up straight when he remembered. Then he realized.

He knew what had happened to Holly's fish.

He looked through the dictionary a little longer.

There was something else he wanted to find.

Then he snapped the book shut.

"I'm going out," he told Holly.

"What about your et-pay tory-say?" she asked.

It took a minute for him to figure it out.

"Later," he said. "I've got to go over to Dawn Bosco's right away."

Chapter 10

It was Pet Week.

There were creatures all over the place.

Matthew's cat, Barney, was curled up on the science table. He had brought her after all.

Dawn had brought the pencilfish and the rummy-nose.

Holly had lent them to her because she had taken such good care of them.

"I knew they belonged to someone," Dawn had said, "when I found them in the park. I was glad when Beast told me."

Right now, Beast took a look at Linda Lorca's worm.

"Worms tunnel around," she told him. "They make the dirt nice and fluffy."

Beast nodded. He kept watching the door.

Something was going to happen.

Something wonderful.

He couldn't wait.

He looked around at the other creatures.

Timothy had brought a fish too.

It was a plain-looking thing.

And Noah was out sick. They'd probably never get to see his ferret.

"Quiet down," Ms. Rooney said for the tenth time.

She wasn't saying that to the class.

She was saying it to Mr. Schaeffer, her cat.

He kept trying to climb up on her head.

Someone screamed behind Beast.

It was Jill Simon.

She was wearing that net thing over her head.

She had on her mother's long white gloves.

"I think Itchy escaped!" she yelled. "I hope he isn't in my desk."

Beast went back to look at her ant farm.

There was a hole in the cover.

An ant was climbing out.

He poked them back in for her. Then he watched as she put her book on top.

"I'm giving the whole farm to Dawn Bosco," she said, "as soon as Pet Week is over. They're too much trouble. I'm just glad to have Goldie, my fish."

Just then the classroom door opened.

It was Mr. Mancina, the principal.

He was carrying a cage. A towel covered most of it.

Beast took a breath.

He couldn't wait for what was going to happen next.

"Glad you're here," said Ms. Rooney. She tried to get Mr. Schaeffer off her shoulder. "Ouch, his claws are sharp."

"For climbing trees," said Mr. Mancina.

Ms. Rooney laughed. "For climbing people too."

Mr. Mancina put the cage down on Ms. Rooney's desk. "Here's the surprise," he said.

Everyone raced up to the front.

Matthew tried to peek under the towel.

"No fair," said Mr. Mancina. "You have to tell me what it is."

"It's a Cavia," said Timothy.

"Right," said Mr. Mancina. "But what's a Cavia?"

Beast waited a moment.

He bet no one knew the answer.

But he did.

"It's a guinea pig," he said.

Mr. Mancina looked surprised. So did Ms. Rooney.

"I knew you'd get it, Beast," said Matthew.

Now Beast was surprised.

He would never have gotten it without Holly and her dictionary.

Mr. Mancina handed Beast the prize. "It's a book," he said. "A book about pets."

"Neat," said Beast.

He had figured it would be something like that.

He was going to read it anyway.

Mr. Mancina pulled the towel off the cage.

Inside was a furry little creature with brown eyes.

Everyone watched him for a while.

Everyone except Beast.

He went back to his seat.

He felt good.

Wonderful.

As smart as Timothy and Noah.

And another thing.

He had brought the best pet.

He had figured it out last night.

He leaned over his desk.

He gave Kissie Poo a pat.

Kissie Poo growled a little. Then she thumped her tail and went back to sleep.

The Polk Street
Guide to Pets

"Circle time," said Ms. Rooney.

Beast grabbed his chair. Everyone was racing to sit in a circle with the teacher.

"We're going to talk about—" Ms. Rooney began.

"Pets," said Timothy.

"Right," said Ms. Rooney.

Beast frowned. Timothy knew everything.

"I'm going to have a hundred pets when I grow up," Beast said before Timothy could say another word.

"No good," Timothy said.

Now what? Beast thought.

Ms. Rooney was nodding. "I think Timothy is right."

"Me too," said Dawn. "Pets need a lot of care. You have to keep them clean. You have to feed them."

"Don't forget love," said Emily. "If you have a hundred pets, when will you have time to talk to them, and pet them, and—"

"Take them to the vet if they're sick," said Jill.

Matthew was laughing. "How would you like to clean up a hundred litter boxes?"

"Yucks," said Jill.

Ms. Rooney picked up a piece of chalk. She wrote RESPONSIBILITY on the chalkboard.

Now everyone was nodding. "You know a cat can live to be sixteen," Emily said. "If you have a cat, you have to think about taking care of it all that time."

"That's a responsibility," Ms. Rooney said.

Beast thought about Kissie Poo. She

wanted to take a walk every two seconds. She'd turn her water dish over and bang it all over the place if the water wasn't fresh. And there was that time she had gotten sick on the rug.

"Yep," Matthew said. "It's a big job to take care of a pet."

"When I grow up," Beast said, "I'm having only one. Two at the most."

"That's what I figured," Timothy said.

"Unless they're worms," said Matthew. "Then you might have a hundred."

Ms. Rooney smiled. "Now, how about some reports on pets . . ."

Hamsters by Alex Walker

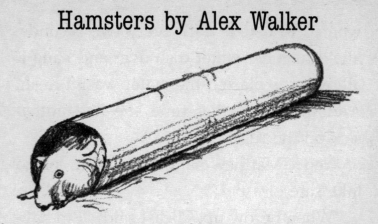

My hamster looks like a teddy bear with fat cheeks. That's because he saves extra food in his cheeks for a snack later on. He's golden brown with tiny ears, and he fits in my hand.

Hamsters make good friends. I talk to mine as much as I can. He likes the sound of my voice, I think, especially when I talk softly. When I pick him up, I move my hand slowly so he isn't afraid.

I touch him when he's sleeping. He doesn't like to be surprised . . . and his teeth are sharp.

His cage is in a warm spot, away from the sun and drafts. I bought it at a pet store. It fits on my desk, and it looks like a city.

It's made of two small cages with a tunnel in between.

The cages are made of wire so he has plenty of air. He sleeps in one spot and eats in another.

The bottoms of the cages have piles of clean wood chips. He loves to hide underneath them.

Sometimes he almost disappears.

Hamsters like to play. You have to find things for them to play with . . . otherwise they're bored and sad.

They like to hide inside cardboard rolls from paper towels. They like to climb and chew on pieces of hard wood. And they love to investigate small boxes.

My hamster is crazy about the exercise wheel. He races on it . . . all night, it seems. Sometimes the squeaking of the wheel wakes me.

If he starts throwing chips out of the cage, I know he's bored. Then I have to find new toys for him.

I buy hamster food at the pet store. I put it in a feeding dish in his cage. But he needs to eat other things too: fruit and vegetables. He loves lettuce, and carrots, and any vegetables my mother is making for supper. His favorites are apples and bananas. He loves a grape or a piece of orange too.

I make sure the water in his sipper bottle is fresh every day.

Warning: My hamster loves to escape. If the cage isn't closed tightly, or if I let him out and don't watch . . . he's gone! Once he managed to get behind the wall. My father had to make holes in the wall to get him out.

Mr. Mancina Talks About
Guinea Pigs

I call them by their real name: *Cavia porcellus.*

They don't look like pigs, but they sound like them, making grunts and squeals. The Cavia in Room 113 has a dark, wiry coat. He peers up at you . . . through hair that almost covers his eyes.

He was easy to tame. He loves the children. Sometimes he sits on Beast's desk and watches him work.

I made a cage for our guinea pig with

wire sides. It's about fifteen inches by twenty inches. We spread wood chips on the bottom and put fresh ones in once a week.

A covered box is in one corner of the cage. He climbs in to take a nap. He feels safe, and he likes to sleep in the dark.

He has his own water sipper and a new, heavier feed dish. (He kept tipping the first one over.) He's messy, so we clean and change both the sipper and the food dish every day.

Like Alex's hamster, he likes to chew on hardwood branches. He scratches his nails on them to keep them trimmed.

Like Alex's hamster, he eats green, leafy vegetables too, and apples and grapes. He'll even eat a tiny bit of leftover whole-wheat bread. You can buy rabbit pellets for him if you like.

Dawn and Jill Tell About Ant Farms

You can use any container for an ant farm. Make sure it has glass sides so you can see what the ants are doing. (The narrower the container, the more you can see.)

Don't forget to cover the top and tape the edges. You don't want your pets to wander away.

Fill the container with dirt.

To find an ant nest, look for ant holes in your yard or turn over a board.

Put a piece of candy or other sweet food nearby. Watch the ants march out to get it.

When a bunch of ants begin to eat the candy, scoop them into the container with a tablespoon.

To feed the ants, give them a tiny, tiny bit of honey mixed with a drop of water.

They like a piece of fruit or a seed or two.

We're sorry, but they won't be your best friend like Kissie Poo or Matthew's Barney. They're friendly to each other, though. They feel each other with their antennae. It looks as if they're talking to each other.

They're hard workers. They dig tunnels all over the place. When they find food, they bring it into the nest to share.

Holly Thinks Tropical Fish Are the Greatest

I don't just think so, I know so.

Get a tank for your birthday. Make sure you get a top too. Otherwise dust might fall into the tank . . . or worse, the fish might jump out.

It's very important to set the tank up and fill it with water and plants a few days before you buy the fish. This gives the plants a chance to root and the water a chance to age.

You'll need to think about light and heat too. Ask the person in the fish store to help you pick the right kinds for your tank.

The most fun is choosing the fish. Guppies are terrific. They're easy and they have lots of babies.

Make sure to buy some plants that float on top of the tank. The babies can hide in the leaves. (Bad news: Sometimes their parents eat them . . . and so do the other fish in the tank.)

Guppies like to eat once or twice a day. You can buy their food at the pet store. Usually they eat dried food, but once in a while you might buy daphnia (water fleas).

Give the guppies only as much as they can eat in about five minutes. It's better to give them too little than too much.

Linda Lorca Loves Worms

It's interesting to have a pet worm . . .
and unusual too. Not too many people
have worms . . . and most people have
never really thought about how worms
live.

You might be surprised to know that there are almost two thousand types of worms in the world. One that was found in Africa was as long as our classroom.

Worms are wonderful. They wiggle through the earth making little tunnels. The dirt becomes light and airy, instead of packed down and hard.

To start a worm world, fill a tall jar with soil. Remember that worms like cool, damp places. You have to keep the jar cool and damp. (Don't drown your worms with too much water.)

Gently put a couple of worms on top of the jar. You'll see them begin to tunnel deep into the soil.

They'll come up at night to feed. Just sprinkle a little oatmeal and a few old leaves on top every couple of weeks.

They'll eat that, and munch on some of the soil too.

Ladybugs by Sherri Dent

I keep my ladybugs in my brother's old aquarium. I keep the top covered. (Once I forgot and they all flew away.)

Ladybugs like to eat leaves. I try to find leaves with stems and tiny twigs. They like to crawl underneath while they're having a snack.

They like water too. Spray the leaves every day.

Their main food is a tiny insect called an aphid. You can find aphids in your garden, on rosebushes and other plants.

A ladybug eats about thirty or forty aphids every day . . . so you'll be busy.

When you do find an aphid, cut the stem

it's on. Put the aphid and stem in a jar of water. More will appear soon. You'll be able to grow aphids and keep your lady-bugs healthy.

Beast Loves Dogs

I guess you're not surprised that I picked a dog. I couldn't pick anything else because Kissie Poo would feel sad.

A dog is a big responsibility. She can live to be old, twelve or fifteen maybe.

Sometimes she gets to be messy-looking. You have to love her even if the hair on her tail falls out.

Here's how to take care of a dog. She should have a nice place to sleep. It can be a clean box with a soft towel. (I read that

somewhere. Kissie Poo doesn't sleep in a box. She sleeps on my bed. She growls if I move my feet one inch.)

When she was a puppy, I fed her three times a day. Now that she's grown up, she eats twice a day. My mother buys hard dog

food and soft dog food. We keep a bowl of water for Kissie Poo on the kitchen floor. We clean the bowl and her food dish every day.

We take Kissie Poo to the vet sometimes. She needs checkups and shots. Sometimes she needs vitamins.

Ask your mom to call the vet to find out what your dog needs.

You can teach a dog to do tricks. Here's how to teach her to come to you.

Put her on one side of the kitchen.

Go to the other side. Say "Come."

Keep doing this until she comes.

Then pet her like crazy. Tell her she's great.

Do it about a hundred times.

She'll get the idea.

You'll be worn out.

Matthew Talks About Cats

You know my cat, Barney. I'll tell you right away that she won't learn tricks. She does mostly just what she wants, but sometimes she comes when I call her.

The good things about her are that she's very clean. She's always washing her fur, and as soon as I showed her the litter box, she was housebroken in two minutes.

She purrs when she's happy. She likes me to talk to her and pet her. She'll scratch if I touch her stomach, and she doesn't like it if I pet her fur in the wrong direction.

One thing she loves to do is sharpen her claws. She'll sharpen them on the furniture unless she has a scratching post.

She likes a warm, dry bed. She eats dry cat food and drinks milk, and we leave a water dish for her in the kitchen.

She jumps up on the sink and tastes the drips from the faucet, but my mother scolds her when she does that.

When she was a kitten we fed her three times a day. Now we feed her twice. Besides the cat food, we give her some fish without bones, and meat, and cooked vegetables. We cut everything up small.

Barney hates peas. We tried to fool her by putting a pea under her fish.

She ate everything but the pea!

Just like dogs, cats need to go to the vet for checkups and shots.

Kittens can be a problem. Ask your vet about an operation so your cat won't have babies. It's sad when there are too many kittens with no one to care for them. (Timothy told me that the male operation is called neutering. The female operation is called spaying. Dogs can have it too.)

The last thing I want to say is that a cat shouldn't wander around outside. She could easily be hit by a car.

Derrick Grace Likes Mice

Don't get just one mouse. He'll be lonely. Get two!

Mice come in different colors. Sometimes they're white with pink eyes. Sometimes they're spotted.

They can live for about two years.

Buy your mice from a clean pet store. They should be five or six weeks old when you bring them home.

You'll need a large mouse cage. It should be about eighteen inches long, nine inches wide, and ten inches high.

Put two inches of wood shavings on the bottom.

A water bottle should hang inside. The water should be changed every day.

Make sure to keep the cage away from the sun or strong light.

Feed your mice birdseed and a little dry dog food. Treat them to tiny pieces of celery, and carrots, and sometimes lettuce. Ask the person in the pet store for exact amounts.

There should always be food in the cage, but be sure to change it twice a day.

Buy a piece of wood at the pet store. Mice need to gnaw so their teeth don't grow too long.

Mice like a small box in their cage with a hole for a door. It's a great place for them to hide or take a nap.

It's really important to clean their cage every week. Put the mice in another box. Wash the cage with soap and water. Dry it carefully.

Don't forget to be kind to your mice. Talk to them softly, and handle them gently.

The Whole Class Loves Skinks

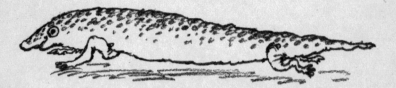

Our skink is as long and skinny as a pencil. He looks like a brown lizard.

In nature, the skink lives in rocky places. If an enemy grabs his tail, he drops it off . . . and grows a new one after he escapes.

We've tried to make our skink feel at home in his tank. We've spread sawdust on the bottom and put in a couple of rocks for him to hide behind.

We feed him live crickets and always keep a few pieces of sliced potatoes in the tank for moisture.

Ms. Rooney says:

Whatever pet you choose, be kind, take good care of it . . . and read books about it.

And Beast says:

You can even find out how to spell your pet's name in the dictionary!

About the Author/About the Artist

Patricia Reilly Giff is the author of more than fifty books for young readers, including the Kids of the Polk Street School books, the Lincoln Lions Marching Band books, and the Polka Dot Private Eye books. She lives in Weston, Connecticut.

Blanche Sims has illustrated all the Polk Street books. She lives in Westport, Connecticut.